Your Dog Might Be a Werewolf, Your Toes Could All Explode

Your Dog Might Be a Werewolf, Your Toes Could All Explode

by David Greenberg

Illustrated by George Ulrich

A BANTAM SKYLARK BOOK

NEW YORK • TORONTO • LONDON • SYDNEY • AUCKLAND

RL 2, 005-008

YOUR DOG MIGHT BE A WEREWOLF, YOUR TOES COULD ALL EXPLODE
A Bantam Skylark Book / February 1992

ISBN 0-553-15909-7

Published simultaneously in the United States and Canada

Bantam Books are published by Bantam Books, a division of Bantam
Doubleday Dell Publishing Group, Inc. Its trademark, consisting of the
words "Bantam Books" and the portrayal of a rooster, is Registered
in U.S. Patent and Trademark Office and in other countries. Marca
Registrada. Bantam Books, 666 Fifth Avenue, New York, New York
10103.

PRINTED IN THE UNITED STATES OF AMERICA

OPM   0 9 8 7 6 5 4 3 2 1

To Sam, Daddy's most beloved honeydrop
—Daddy

Frankie and Peter Struthers
Were opposite sorts of brothers:

Frankie would climb to the top of a tree
And then he'd recklessly jump

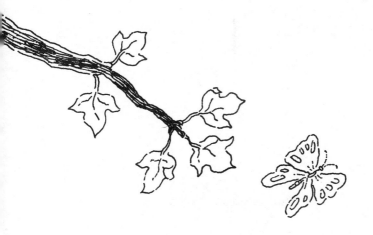

While Peter felt certain he'd break his neck
Falling off a stump

Frankie would skip through a graveyard
Under the full moon bright
While Peter couldn't fall asleep
Without the hallway light

Peter was short
While Frankie was tall
Peter read books
While Frankie played ball
Peter worried the worsest worries
While Frankie said he didn't at all

Oh, Peter was
a worrier
He worried
about this
and that
He worried he
was much
too skinny
He worried he
was much
too fat

He worried that he'd go to school
And forget to zip his fly
He worried that his belly button
Might suddenly untie

"I'm w-w-worried" said Peter
And Frankie said "Harumph
Snakes got whiskers, dogs are purry
Frogs got feathers, fish are furry
Big kids never ever worry"

But Peter couldn't help it
He feared his toes would explode
That he'd kiss his mom good night
And change into a toad

That he might be hit by a meteorite
(Someone's bound to be hit)
He thought of poisonous spiders
And worried he'd get bit

Peter Struthers imagined
He'd grow an elephant trunk
Worries leave no time for study
He worried that he'd flunk

"I'm w-w-worried" said Peter
And Frankie said "Harumph
Snakes got whiskers, dogs are purry
Frogs got feathers, fish are furry
Big kids never ever worry"

But Peter Struthers bit his nails
And worried he might get zits

That his dog could be a werewolf
About to chomp him to bits

And he worried he'd go to school
And forget to wear any clothes
He was positive that boogers
Were hanging from his nose

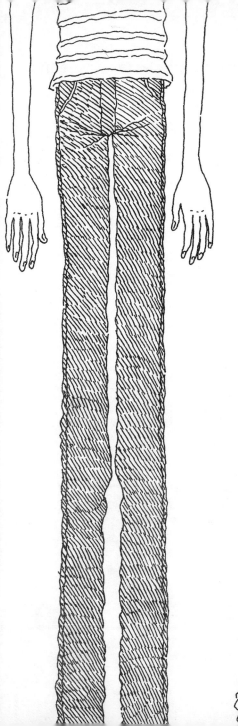

And he feared
he was much
too tall
About to grow
much taller
And he fussed
he was much
too short
About to grow
much smaller

And he worried that people were whispering
About his terrible breath
And he worried that he worried too much
That he'd worry himself to death

"I'm w-w-worried" said Peter
And Frankie said "Harumph
Snakes got whiskers, dogs are purry
Frogs got feathers, fish are furry
Big kids never ever worry"

But Peter pulled at his hair
(Was it prematurely gray?)
He worried if he jumped
That he'd simply float away

And he dreaded he'd never be chosen
To play on any team
That everything he thought was real
Might really be a dream

And the next time he flew in an airplane
Peter felt for sure
Instead of the door to the bathroom
He'd open the exit door

Or he'd fall asleep in his soup
And then of course he'd drown
Or next time on the toilet
A hand would pull him down

"I'm w-w-worried" said Peter
And Frankie said "Harumph
Snakes got whiskers, dogs are purry
Frogs got feathers, fish are furry
Big kids never ever worry"

And suddenly Peter stopped
A thought popped into his head
A unique and terrible worry
And he turned to Frankie and said

"I've just had an awesome worry
A worry entirely new
I'm sorry to say it won't go away
For this worry I worry's for you"

"Don't be weird" said Frankie
"Your worries are dorky and dumb
But just for the sake of brotherly love
I guess I'll listen some"

"Never mind" said Peter
"I really hate to bore you"
"No no no" Frankie replied
"It's not boring, I assure you"

"You're much too kind" said Peter
"I've really got to go"
But Frankie grabbed at his collar
"First I want to know"

"OK" said Peter "I'm worried
There's a shark in your water bed
And tonight when you go to sleep
He'll gobble off your head"

"I'm w-w-worried" said Peter
And Frankie said "Harumph
Snakes got whiskers, dogs are purry
Frogs got feathers, fish are furry
Big kids never ever worry"

But then as bedtime grew closer
As day turned into night
Frankie began to think
"What if Peter is right?"

"What if he's truly correct
And a shark is in my bed
Why, he'd chomp me all to pieces
And I would wake up dead"

"Why, he'd grind up my liver
Suck out my veins
Swallow my eyeballs
Pluck out my brains"

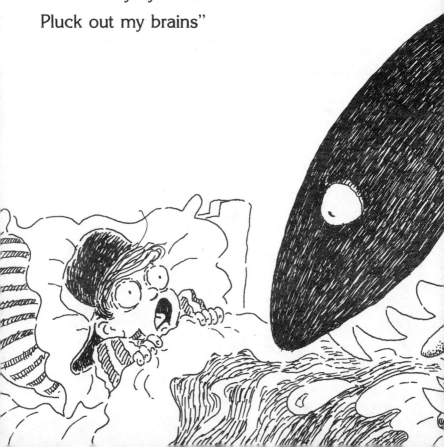

And Frankie Struthers
Fretted and fussed
Shivered and quivered
Sweated and cussed

And his body started changing
His skin got rough and rubbery
He started shrinking and shriveling
His shape became more blubbery

And he soon looked like a meatball
The greasy grimy sort
Yes, Frankie Struthers had turned
Into a WORRY WART!!!

And all of his toes exploded
In a thunderous flash of light
And his dog changed into a werewolf
And started to snarl and bite

And glancing down he saw
He'd forgotten to zip his fly
And fearless Frankie Struthers
Started to sniffle and cry

"I'm w-w-worried" said Frankie
And Peter said "Harumph
Snakes got whiskers, dogs are purry
Frogs got feathers, fish are furry
Warts like you never worry"

And though his dog was howling
And his brother turned into a wart
Peter simply yawned
"I'm not the worrying sort"

Yes, Peter never worried again
"It's too dangerous to risk it"
And Frankie? Well, a shark in his bed
It swallowed him like a biscuit.

About the Author

DAVID GREENBERG is the author of *Slugs*, *Teaching Poetry to Children*, and the Bantam Skylark book *The Great School Lunch Rebellion*. He travels to schools and conferences around the country, speaking about writing and education, reading his poetry, and participating in writing workshops and education forums. Raised in New York, he currently lives in Portland, Oregon, with his wife, Sharon, his sons, Justin, Ryan, and Sam, a Fiendish Feline named Snowy, and other carnivores too numerous to mention.

About the Illustrator

GEORGE ULRICH was born in Morristown, New Jersey, and received his bachelor of fine arts from Syracuse University. He has illustrated a number of Bantam Skylark books, including *Make Four Million Dollars by Next Thursday!* by Stephen Manes, *The Amazing Adventure of Me, Myself, and I* by Jovial Bob Stine, and the Never Sink Nine series by Gibbs Davis. Mr. Ulrich lives in Marblehead, Massachusetts, with his wife and two sons.